MW00874488

Tawanda's Tales: Best Friends Forever is dedicated to my husband, Rob, who was willing to accept another crazy dream of mine as his own and pushed me to "go for it".

To my daughters-may they continue to have the free loving, fun personalities that they have and hopefully have a little tamer adventures than Tawanda and Tate.

To my parents-who I am sure are a little fearful of what other adventures Tawanda may have taken in her early years.

To my friend Tara-who was literally by my side for most adventures from age 6 and beyond.

To my friends and family that read rough draft after rough draft of my story and pushed me to keep going.

And lastly...

To my Honey Horse that taught me how to ride, took us on many wild adventures, and was a great friend that kept many of my deep, dark secrets growing up on Glass Avenue.

"Be careful, no horse buttin' around, and NO motorized vehicles!" said Tawanda's Dad as he and her mom jumped in the truck to go out for the night with Aunt Cindy and Uncle Larry. This was a typical Friday night occurrence, but this night was extra special because it was Dad's birthday so they would be out a little later than usual.

Lil'
Rudd
Express

"Ok! Sounds good! We are just going to watch our movies." Tawanda said with a glimmer in her eye and a glance at her best friend, Tate. Dad always gave the same list of rules each time he left the farm. Tawanda had been hearing that same list of rules for as long as she could remember.

Once the truck engine started, Tate and Tawanda ran over to peek out the huge picture window of Tawanda's house on Glass Avenue. Her house sat at the bottom of a slight hill and when Tate and Tawanda saw the bumper of that shiny, red truck pass over the hill and out of sight they looked at each other, smiled, and jumped up off of the floor.

"I'll grab the lead rope," said Tate.
"I'll go holler at Honey," said Tawanda.
And out the back door of the house they ran.

Honey!
Here
Ho-nn-ee-yy!

A beautiful golden palomino quarter horse came running up to the front pasture gate where Tawanda was standing. "Hey, Honey Horse, you are such a good friend to me. You always keep all of my secrets, just like a best friend should. I hope you are ready for some fun!"

"Hi Kathy! I am so glad we were able to meet to go out for supper tonight for Kenny's birthday," said Cindy.
"Me, too," said Kathy. "I am ready for a calm, relaxing evening."
"What are the kids doing tonight?" asked Uncle Larry.
"Oh, it worked out perfect, the boys are helping Cork bale hay and Tawanda invited her friend Tate over; they rented movies to watch while we are gone."

"I found the lead rope," Tate said as she ran towards Tawanda and Honey.
"Awesome, let's go!"
Tawanda clipped the lead rope on Honey's halter and led her out the gate. Once they were outside the gate Tawanda led Honey beside a tall, white wooden fence while Tate pushed Honey's backside towards the fence. Honey was trying to move away from the fence almost like she had heard Dad's warning before he left.

Once Tawanda had climbed up on the trusty palomino mare, Tate grabbed Tawanda's leg with one hand and wrapped her other hand in Honey's mane and used it like a ladder to climb up the horse. Tate quickly found her spot on Honey's back. "Let's rock and roll!"

Into the hayfield the threesome of friends went and the wild, speedy adventure on Glass Avenue began. The girls and Honey lined up in their "usual" starting spot in the grassy field and waited for a car to come roaring over the hill.

"Here comes one!" said Tate.
"Let's do it!" said Tawanda. She made a kissing noise with her mouth and off Honey went, thundering down the field. Honey's hooves were pounding on the ground so hard that dust was billowing up behind them.
Tate was squealing and holding on to Tawanda as tight as she could, "I bet this is just like running in the derby!"
A car that was passing by slowed down to watch the wild girls on the horse.

"YAHOO, we beat them!" Tawanda screamed while giggling and pulling back on the lead rope that she was using as reins.

Here comes another one yelled Tate and off they went barreling down to the other end of the hayfield, racing another car. "This time let's jump," said Tawanda.

"You got it!" yelled Tate.

As they were approaching the end of the field, Tate grabbed onto Tawanda's belt loops and in one big swoop both girls came tumbling off of Honey's side. Honey slid to a halt just like a champion reining horse. The girls rolled around in the sweet smelling alfalfa, laughing, and rubbing parts of their bodies that were a little sore from their dismount.

Ice Cream

"This has been a great celebration," said Kenny. "Nothing like the steakhouse and some ice cream to make a birthday night complete."

"Good food does take time, but it sure is worth it, isn't it?" said Larry.

"We should probably be heading home, though, it's getting late and the girls did only get two movies to watch. They are probably almost done with both," said Kathy.

As the sun started to set in the summer sky and after several races with cars on Glass Avenue, the girls decided it was time to put Honey away and call it a day.

"Thanks for all of the fun, Honey Horse! I bet Dad doesn't know you are faster than that motorized vehicle he is always telling us not to drive," Tawanda said with a laugh and a pat on Honey's strong neck. "Thanks for being one of my best friends, Honey."

Honey neighed as if to say you are welcome and thank YOU girls for the fun as she pranced over to the water tank to get a long drink of water.

"Good girl," said Tate. "You deserve a cool drink after all of that running."

As the girls walked towards the house giggling and comparing scrapes from their many dismounts, they heard the rumble of a familiar truck slowing down to turn in the driveway.

"Hurry, get in the house!" yelled Tawanda
"Quick turn on the television. Cover up! Don't let them see that rip in your pants," hollered Tate. The girls scurried to get under the blankets and on the couch.

"Hi girls! How was your night?" asked Mom as she kissed the top of their heads.
Are the movies good?" asked Dad.
"Yes, the first one was real good!" said Tate.
"This one is hilarious," said Tawanda.
Mom smiled and told them good night.
As mom walked away, she had a smile on her face thinking about what a nice, calm night the girls must have had watching movies.
As dad walked away he paused, looked at the screen and realized that the movie was just beginning. He also noticed Tawanda's dirty pant leg hanging out from under the blanket.
"Hope you girls had a good night watching movies and were careful!" he said as he walked down the hallway with raised eyebrows.

"Good night, Tawanda!"
"Good night, Tate!"
"I can't wait for our next adventure," said Tawanda.
"Me either."
"Best friends forever?"
"Forever!" Tate said with a grin.

Jennifer Schmitt was born and raised in rural Iowa. She is a country girl, beef lover, wife, mom of two girls, and a special education consultant. Jennifer enjoys writing stories that include bits and pieces of her childhood memories and the new memories she is making with her own children. She loves hiding little hints of rural Iowa within her books, some of those hidden things may be little small town secrets, but some may be nationally known. When Jennifer isn't working at her day job you can find her spending time outdoors with her family on their farm in Iowa or blogging at www.tailsfromthegravelroad.com.

Illustrator Bio:
C.J. Love is a 2008 MICA (Maryland Institute College of Art) graduate and has a BFA in Graphic Design. He specializes in illustration, digital illustration, caricatures, mural painting, logo design, prototype drawing, and illustrating children's books. C.J. is also a top pro on Thumbtack. Please visit his website to see more of his work, It's **www.clove2design.com**.

To those reading the book aloud:

I have compiled some questions that may help when reading the book aloud to help with building vocabulary and comprehension skills with children in your home or classroom.

After page 4: What do you think is going to happen in this story? Why did Dad sound concerned?

After page 6: Make a prediction-Who is Honey?

After page 8: Why would a horse be a good friend to share secrets with in real life?

While reading age 14: What does the word billowing mean? How did you figure out the meaning of the word? What do you think the people in the car were thinking when they drove by the girls?

After page 20: What does the word scurried mean?

After page 23: Do you think Dad knew what had gone on while he was gone?

After page 25: Based on the illustration on this page, what do you predict will be Tawanda's next adventure?

Extension options:

- Write a different ending to the story

- Based on the illustration on page 25, write about Tawanda's next adventure

Dream big and huge~

Jen

Made in the USA
Columbia, SC
13 February 2019